New Pebbledown

Pier

Nipper To The Rescue

PAT POSNER

Illustrated by
Strawberrie Donnelly

BLOOMSBURY
CHILDREN'S
BOOKS

First published in Great Britain in 1998
Bloomsbury Publishing Plc, 38 Soho Square, London, W1V 5DF

A CIP catalogue record of this book is available from the
British Library

ISBN 0 7475 3854 9

Printed in England by Clays Ltd, St Ives plc

10 9 8 7 6 5 4 3 2 1

Cover design by Michelle Radford

One

'We could sleep in the lighthouse,' said Molly.

'What! And climb up all those twisty stairs every night?' Gran Hinglepot shook her head.

'Your scarf must be as tall as the lighthouse, Gran,' said Molly. 'We could lower it down from the lantern deck, then you could tie it under your arms and we'd pull you up!'

Gran sucked her breath in through the gap in her front teeth as she gazed at her scarf. The end nearest her was attached to an enormous wooden knitting needle, the far end of it was coiled round and round in a huge heap in the well part of an old fishing dinghy. The dinghy had been sunk into the floor, at one side of the fireplace, by a fisherman who'd once lived in the cottage. *He'd* used it to keep his big fishing net in.

Mum Hinglepot had wanted to keep coal and driftwood for the fire in the sunken dinghy. But Gran had claimed it for her scarf. Gran often got her own way!

'It would probably stretch your scarf quite a bit, Gran, if we used it to pull you up to the lantern deck,' Molly continued.

'Stretching it to make it longer would be cheating,' said Gran. 'Anyway,' she snorted, 'I am not sleeping in the lighthouse!'

'What about sleeping in the cave in our secret cove?' suggested Jack.

'The cave is much too small for five

people, Jack,' said Dad Hinglepot. 'We'd
all suffocate in our sleep.'

'Tents then,' said Molly. 'We'll sleep in
tents in the garden.'

Molly knew it was a silly idea as soon as
she'd suggested it. Bray and Blare, the
beach donkeys, slept in a stable in the
garden. But they were always breaking out
and going in search of their best friends,
the Hinglepots.

'Sleep in a tent and be woken up by a donkey wanting to share my sleeping bag!' said Gran. 'I'd rather drown in my bed.'

'The rain would soak its way through the tent canvas anyway,' said Dad. 'Water dripping through a tent would be even worse than all this rain dripping through our cottage roof.'

'Well, Jack and I could sleep in the old stable,' said Molly. 'Then –'

'Then someone would report it to the "cruelty to children place",' Gran said darkly. 'Or to the RSPCA. *They'd* think it was cruel making donkeys share a stable with you two!'

Molly ignored Gran's interruption and continued, 'Then you and Mum could go and sleep at Cousin Ezra's, Dad, and –'

'If ever I set foot in Ezra's Junk Shop it will be over my drowned body!' Dad retorted. 'And he is not your cousin. He's

your mother's three-times-removed
cousin. But . . .' Dad took a deep breath.

'. . . We'll all be drowned bodies if it
keeps raining like this,' he gabbled.
'Nobody comes to our part of the beach
when it rains so there's nobody to take
photographs of and nobody to sell
photographs to . . . Pedro isn't paying us
rent for the donkeys' field and stabling
because nobody comes to our end of the

beach to ride his donkeys when it's raining so he isn't earning any money to pay us with . . . so that means we haven't any money to live on, let alone fix the holes in the roof where the rain's coming in.'

'Speaking so fast will make your jawbones lock together, Harold!' Gran scolded.

Molly waited to see if Dad's jawbones would get locked together. They didn't. But his nose woffled. It woffled so much that he looked like a crazy rabbit.

'The eggs!' he shouted, leaping up and running towards the kitchen. '*Slonkingpod!* I've burnt the boiled eggs.'

Molly and Jack grinned in delight as they followed Dad into the kitchen. This was the best thing that had happened all day! Not the eggs getting burnt but Dad saying that word. Because that meant . . . a fine!

Two

Gran marched into the kitchen after them, the far end of the scarf uncoiling itself behind her. 'Three rows of knitting, Harold!' said Gran, thrusting her knitting into his hands.

Some people have special boxes to put money in every time they say a naughty word. The Hinglepots had Gran's scarf. Not to put money in. To knit! Gran wanted her scarf long enough to get a mention in the Book of Records.

But Gran hated knitting. So the family had to help. A naughty word meant one row of knitting. A very naughty word meant two rows of knitting. A *really* naughty word like *'slonkingpod'* meant three rows of knitting.

'What about the eggs?' said Dad, glancing towards the smoking pan on the stove.

'I'll see to them,' said Gran, turning the stove off with one hand and wrapping a tea-towel round the pan handle with the other. 'I don't know how a son of mine can be so blether-headed that he can't even boil eggs,' she continued, as she opened the window and threw the smoking pan out.

'In, over, through, off,' murmured Dad as he worked the chunky wool over the needles. 'You are not going to make me say another naughty word by calling me names,' he told Gran.

Gran grinned toothily; sometimes it worked. Sometimes she could make

Harold so mad that he'd say four or five
naughty words in one go – that meant he
had to knit at least a dozen rows.

'Where's your mother anyway?' Dad
asked irritably, glaring towards Jack and
Molly. 'It was her turn to make supper.'

'She's gone round to Cousin Ezra's to
paint sand,' Molly told him.

'Ezra Junk is not your cousin,' Dad said

again. 'He's your mother's three-times-removed cousin.'

'If Ezra's grandfather's fortune had turned up, Ezra would have been Emma's three-times-removed *wealthy* cousin,' said Gran.

Dad snorted. 'The missing fortune is a figment of Ezra's imagination. We all know he's crazy.'

'Emma will end up as crazy as Ezra if she keeps spending so much time with him in that Junk Shop,' chortled Gran. 'I mean, who in their right mind would paint sand?'

'It's for putting into cars,' Jack said.

'Are you telling me that your mother is painting sand to put into cars?' Dad felt so bewildered he dropped a stitch. 'Oh, *chinkle*,' he said.

'That's another row of knitting, Harold!' Gran said happily.

'Not real cars, Dad. Clear plastic ones,' Molly explained. 'Mum and Cousin Ezra are filling them with layers of different coloured sand.'

'Then Cousin Ezra is going to paint "*A present from Pebbledown Bay*" on them,' said Jack. 'They're going to be holiday souvenirs. To sell in his shop. Half the money from selling the souvenirs will be Mum's. She says she'll use it to get the roof fixed. And,' he continued, 'Cousin Ezra is going to use his half to buy a house in a city where there're lots of people around all the time. Fancy wanting to move away from Pebbledown Bay to go and live in a city! Living in a city is horrible!'

'Lots of traffic, lots of noise, crowded streets, not being allowed out on our own – apart from going to a crowded school on a crowded bus,' said Molly with a shudder.

'We'll have to move back to the city if we don't earn some money soon,' said Dad.

Dad Hinglepot often said things he didn't really mean when he was in what his family called a 'gloomy-doomy mood'. But, this time, he meant what he'd said!

Molly and Jack stared at each other in dismay. They couldn't bear the thought of moving back to the city.

The old cottage, with its huge garden at the side, was in a hilly area right above Pebbledown Bay. There was a track behind the cottage that led to the disused lighthouse that Mum and Dad Hinglepot had bought along with the cottage. Mum had a big telescope for star-gazing in the Lantern Tower and Jack and Molly had dens and playrooms in the rest of it.

Near the lighthouse was a narrow path that went all the way down to a long, wide stretch of beach. There was another path,

too, a hidden, twisty path that led to a small creek. They kept a rowing boat there which Jack and Molly used to reach their secret cove where they'd discovered a small cave in the overhanging cliff. Sometimes they rowed past the cove to Pebbledown Island. They'd built a grass hut there, right next to the shallow channel where Susie and Charlie, two friendly seahorses, lived.

'Move from Pebbledown Bay!' they cried. 'But we can't! We love it here.'

'I know we do,' Dad agreed. 'I don't *want* to move back and get a job cleaning sewers again! But when we bought this cottage six months ago we thought I'd be able to earn money selling holiday-makers their photographs. We didn't know it was going to rain all summer and keep everyone away. And we didn't know the roof was going to start leaking like this!'

'Mum said she'd use her half of the souvenir money to get the roof fixed,' Jack reminded Dad.

'There'll be nobody to sell the souvenirs *to* because nobody comes here when it's raining!' Dad reminded Jack.

'There must be something we can do!' said Molly desperately.

Gran didn't want to move from Pebbledown Bay, either. Her scarf had grown much longer since they'd come here. With so many problems there was always someone saying a naughty word. 'What we need is a miracle,' she sighed.

And just then there was a loud hammering at the front door.

Three

When Jack and Molly opened the door, a tall, thin man strode into the hall. His black cloak flapped wetly around his ankles as he walked towards the stairs.

Jack and Molly gazed from the man to the madly-patterned cases he'd dumped on the hall floor.

Dad came into the hall trailing Gran's scarf behind him. 'In, over, through . . .' His voice tailed off as he gazed at the stranger.

The man introduced himself: 'Miracle the Miraculous Magician,' he boomed, twirling his moustache then lifting his top hat with one finger. 'And you, my good sir? You are . . .?'

'Harold Hinglepot,' replied Dad. 'Can't shake hands, I'm afraid. They're full of knitting.'

'That's all right. I'll just go to my room.' The magician picked up his cases and walked up three stairs.

'Wait! Wait!' said Dad. 'Where do you think you're going?'

'To my room. The little one at the back, overlooking the sea. Mrs Goodbody saves it for me every year. By the way, where is the good lady?'

'Mrs Goodbody doesn't live here anymore,' said Jack. 'We live here now.'

'Didn't Mrs Goodbody mention me?' asked the magician, his moustache drooping. 'I come to New Pebbledown every year to perform my miraculous magic. Two o'clock at the end of the pier and six o'clock at the Palace Theatre. Every day come rain, hail or shine,' he added.

'And every year,' he continued, 'I come here to Pebbledown Bay where Mrs Goodbody saves me, Miracle, and my cases containing my miraculous magic . . .' he winked at Molly, '. . . the little room at the back, overlooking the sea.'

'The little room at the back, overlooking the sea, is *my* room,' said Gran, who'd joined them in the hall.

'So does that mean that I, Miracle, have nowhere to stay?' asked the magician. He glanced at Molly, before stooping to stroke long fingers over the patterns on his two cases.

As Molly watched, the patterns seemed to turn into words: *Don't send Miracle away!* She blinked and looked again. Nothing but patterns – but she was sure she'd seen the words. 'Gran,' she whispered. 'You said

we needed a miracle. Now we've got one and we can't send him away!'

'But all the rooms have got rain coming through the ceiling,' said Gran. 'He'd have to keep getting up to empty buckets and bowls. You know how quickly they fill up!'

'*Your* buckets and bowls might fill up very quickly,' said Miracle. 'For the time being . . .' he winked at Molly again and she felt all tingly-excited, '. . . I could replace them with my magic pottles. They never get full no matter how much liquid goes into them!'

'Very well,' said Gran, looking up at Miracle. 'You can have my . . . I mean *your* room.'

They all went upstairs, then the Hinglepots' strange-looking guest replaced all the buckets and bowls with strange-looking jugs that he pulled out of one of his cases. 'That's sorted that!' he said. 'How about supper?'

'First we need to sort out where I'm going to sleep,' said Gran.

'You can have my room, Gran,' said Molly. 'I'll sleep in Jack's room on a camp bed.'

They were all sitting round the kitchen table when Mum came in through the back door ten minutes later. Miracle stood up and doffed his top hat, but Mum didn't seem to notice him.

'She's in one of her dreamy moods,' Jack whispered.

Molly leapt up, then drew her mum over to the table. 'Mum!' she said. 'This is Miracle. He's . . . he's a magician,' she continued, excitedly, 'and he's staying here for a while.'

'At your service, good lady!' boomed Miracle, and Molly felt that tingly-excitement again.

'That's nice,' Mum said with a smile. 'What's for supper?'

But there wasn't any supper for Mum. Dad had scrambled the last three eggs for Miracle.

'It's all right,' said Mum. 'I'm sure there's a lettuce leaf or two in the fridge. I'll make do with a lettuce sandwich.'

The second Mum got the lettuce leaves out of the fridge, there was a loud *eee-ore, eee-ore* and Bray and Blare stuck their heads through the kitchen window.

'All right,' sighed Mum. 'I'll share it with you two.'

'But if you three eat all the lettuce what can my rabbit have to eat?' boomed Miracle.

'Rabbit?' asked Jack and Molly. 'Where is it?'

'In my top hat of course. Where else would a magician keep a rabbit?' said Miracle.

He took his top hat off and muttered softly into it.

'Oh, wow!' gasped Molly as something that wasn't a rabbit popped its head over the brim.

Four

'Dabra!' said Miracle. 'All this rain and leaking roofs must have dampened my magic!'

'*Kyow-kyow-kyow!*' cried the something that wasn't a rabbit, popping all the way out of the top hat.

'I'll put up with you having *my* room,' Gran told Miracle. 'But I will not put up with having a seagull on our kitchen table.'

'I'll put it back in my hat and when my hat dries my rabbit will pop out,' said Miracle.

'*Kyow-kyow,*' the seagull said softly, tears trickling down its face.

'Don't put him back in your top hat,'
Molly begged Miracle. 'Let Jack and me
have him. We've always wanted a pet.'
The donkeys didn't count as pets. They
belonged to Pedro.

Molly gazed longingly at the seagull. She
felt sure he wanted to be their pet.

'Very well. He's yours,' said Miracle.
'But take him away so I can't see him. I

don't want to be reminded of failed magic. And don't you dare tell anyone he came out of my top hat.'

The seagull hopped onto Molly's shoulder. She smiled happily at him and hurried out of the room and up the stairs to Jack's bedroom.

Jack followed her. 'Why did you say we'd have him as a pet?' he sighed, sitting down on his bed. 'A seagull is a silly thing to have as a pet.'

'A *magic* seagull isn't,' Molly replied. 'He's got to be magic if he came out of a magician's hat, hasn't he?'

Jack looked doubtfully at the seagull.

The seagull stared mournfully back and flicked his wet feathers. '*Kyow?*' he said. Then he jumped off Molly's shoulder and hopped along Jack's bed until he came to Jack's pillow. He felt under the pillow with his beak and *kyowed* softly before picking up the small towel Jack kept under his pillow to dry his feet when the rain dripping through the hole in the roof made them too wet to bear.

He carried the towel to Molly then hopped onto her lap. '*Kyow*,' he said politely.

'See!' said Molly. 'That proves he's magic! How else would he have known there was a towel under your pillow to dry his feathers?'

Jack was frowning slightly as he watched his sister dry the seagull. The bird couldn't *really* be magic, could it? He shook his head. Of course it couldn't. Besides, he didn't believe in magic. He believed that Miracle was a magician – that was different. Magician's magic was just clever trickery.

The seagull turned its head and looked at Jack. Jack looked back and wriggled uncomfortably; he was almost sure the seagull's eyes had changed to green, then to orange then back to black.

Three days went past. Now, even Molly was beginning to think the seagull wasn't magic. 'Nipper seemed so special, Jack!' she said. She'd called him Nipper because of the way he nipped at Jack's fossils and at the sardines she gave him. 'But, apart from taking the odd paddle in one of the pottles, he doesn't do anything. I really thought he and Miracle were going to help in some way, like making the rain stop,' she added sadly.

When Dad Hinglepot came in, he said the rain was still keeping holiday-makers away. 'We really will have to move back to the city!' he said.

Miracle said the rain didn't stop holiday-makers coming to watch him at the end of the pier at two o'clock every day.

'Rain doesn't stop them coming to watch you because rain doesn't keep them away from New Pebbledown because there's plenty of places where they can shelter from the rain or places they can go to dry off when they're wet. Holiday-makers would come here to our end of the beach if they had somewhere they could go and sit to dry off when they're wet. The only place is Mrs Hinglepot's three-times-removed cousin's miserable shop, but there's too much junk in the way!' gabbled Dad.

Then his face and mouth went very still.

Molly gasped and stared at him in fascinated horror. Gran's warning had come true at last! Dad's jawbones had locked together.

Five

'*Kyow!*' Nipper zoomed from Molly's shoulder to Dad's shoulder. He rubbed his beak around Dad's jawbones then . . . he nipped one of Dad's ears!

'*Slonkingpod!*' yelled Dad. Nipper kyowed and flew into Miracle's top hat.

'Three rows, Harold!' said Gran, thrusting her knitting needles into Dad's hands.

'In, over, through, off. Get that gull out of here!'

'And out of my top hat!' Miracle boomed, tipping Nipper out onto Molly's shoulder.

'That was nearly magic unlocking Dad's jawbones like that,' Molly whispered to Nipper as she hurried upstairs. 'But I wish you'd do some real magic and find a way for us to stay here!'

'*Kyow. But I need a top hat to live in first.*'

Molly stared at Nipper. 'Did I really hear you say you need a top hat to live in?' she asked.

But Nipper just stared at her.

Jack just stared at Molly, too, when she told him what she thought she'd heard. Then he said, 'If you seriously think you heard it . . . go and find him a top hat to live in. Cousin Ezra is sure to have one in his junk shop.'

Mum Hinglepot was there when Jack and Molly, with Nipper on her shoulder, walked into Cousin Ezra's junk shop. She

was pouring brightly-coloured
painted sand into clear plastic cars.

'She's not really with us,' said Cousin
Ezra, greeting Molly and Jack. 'She thinks
she saw an undiscovered comet last night.
It was probably a big drop of rain that
landed on her telescope but . . . she's got
her head in the clouds again.'

That's what they said about Mum when
she went all dreamy.

Molly wasn't interested in Mum's undiscovered comet. She wanted to know if Ezra had a top hat anywhere. 'I think Nipper would feel more at home if he had a top hat to live in,' she said.

'There is one somewhere,' said Ezra. 'It belonged to my grandfather. He promised he'd leave me a fortune. But all he left me was his top hat! It's a lovely hat but it's not worth *that* much!'

'He left you this shop as well,' said Mum suddenly. 'This shop could make you a fortune if you'd use it for something other than junk.'

'My name is Junk. I can't use it for anything else,' said Cousin Ezra.

Molly sighed. They'd heard this argument hundreds of times since they'd come to live in Pebbledown Bay. She pulled Jack over to the junkiest part of the shop. 'Come on,' she said, 'help me find Cousin Ezra's grandfather's top hat.'

Jack sighed and began poking around amongst piles of useless junk.

Molly searched enthusiastically. She was determined to find the top hat for Nipper to live in. She was sure the gull would do something *really* magic then.

'Why don't we get Nipper that cage to live in?' said Jack, pointing to an enormous parrot's cage hanging down from a hook on the ceiling. 'Why's it got to be a top hat?'

Nipper stared beadily at Jack. Jack tried to look away but he couldn't! He felt his legs go all wobbly and he sat down quickly on an old settee. To his surprise, Nipper was perching on the back of it. Jack shivered. He hadn't seen Nipper move from his sister's shoulder. How come he was here?

Then Nipper *kyowed* and fell off the back of the settee.

'Nipper!' Molly leapt up and dashed over. She knelt on the settee and peered anxiously over the back of it. Then she caught her breath in a long 'aah', and, worried in case Nipper was hurt, Jack twisted himself round to kneel up beside his sister.

'Look!' Molly said croakily. 'Nipper's found it! He's found the top hat!'

Molly stretched an arm down to reach the hat and pulled it up with Nipper still sitting on the brim. 'He knew just where to look. I said he was magic, didn't I?' she whispered to Jack.

'Huh!' said Jack, grinning as Nipper put one claw inside the hat and began to scrabble it around. There was nothing magic about that!

'I'd forgotten what a nice hat it was,' said Cousin Ezra, moving towards them. 'I wonder if it fits me?' He held out his hands for the hat, Nipper stopped scrabbling and fluttered onto Molly's shoulder.

'It's too small for you, Ezra!' laughed Mum. 'Let me try it on.'

As Mum lifted the top hat from Ezra's head, Nipper *kyowed* and Jack found himself looking at the seagull. Nipper slowly closed one eye, then opened it again. And, just then, Mum gave a surprised cry.

'There's a little snick in the lining,' she said, 'and there's a piece of paper under it. I'll see if I can pull it out . . .'

'It's an envelope,' said Molly, her eyes on her mum's fingers. 'It must be quite old, it's all yellow. And,' she added, 'there's some writing on the envelope. It's a name. 'Ezra Obadiah Junk'. Is that you?' she asked Cousin Ezra excitedly.

'It is,' he replied. 'And,' he added gloomily, after taking the envelope, 'it's nothing to get excited about. The envelope's too small and flat for anything to be inside.'

But he opened it and dipped his fingers in. And he pulled something out!

Then his face turned red and then white and then green. He stumbled to the settee and lowered himself onto it.

Six

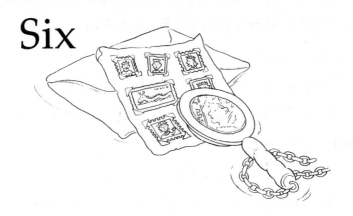

'Grandfather's fortune,' whispered Ezra, gazing down at a sheet of paper covered in stamps. 'He hid it safely away in his top hat.'

Ezra reached for his eye-glass that he wore on a chain around his neck. 'My, my, there are some rare and valuable beauties here. In mint condition too,' he added, and the eye-glass fell from his trembling fingers and plopped against his chest.

'Oh, oh,' he groaned, 'to think they've been there all these years! To think, to think . . .' his eyes started from his face in horror. 'To think I could have sold the top hat to someone!'

'But you didn't,' said Molly. 'You didn't sell it and now, thanks to Nipper, you've found your grandfather's fortune!'

Cousin Ezra's eyes returned to normal. He nodded and patted Molly's hand. 'And now I can sell these stamps and buy a little house in the city, miles away from here.'

'How can you want to move from Pebbledown Bay and go and live in a city?' yelled Jack. 'Gran's right. You're crazy!'

Jack leapt up and stormed out of the shop.

'He's upset because Dad says we'll have to move because it keeps raining and he can't earn any money and we need money to fix our roof because it's leaking,' Molly explained in a rush. 'But we don't want to move. *We* love it here.'

'We certainly don't want to move,' Mum agreed. 'There's something lucky . . . or magical about Pebbledown Bay. I'm on the verge of discovering a new comet, I know I am.'

'You won't have to move now this gull has found Grandfather's fortune!' said Ezra.

'What do you mean, Cousin Ezra?' Molly asked.

'Your mum is always saying Pebbledown Bay needs a café,' replied Ezra, smiling at his three-times-removed cousin.

Mum Hinglepot nodded. 'A café that sells *Milky Way Milk Shakes* in drinking cups that look just like the Big Dipper,' she said.

'Stars again,' muttered Molly. She knew the Milky Way was a galaxy and the Big Dipper was a group of stars that looked

like a long-handled drinking cup.

'Of course, the café would have to sell food as well,' said Mum. 'Like my *Red Giant Pies* and *Star-gazey Puddings* . . .'

'Dad said people would come to Pebbledown Bay, even when it's raining, if they had somewhere to sit and dry off,' said Molly. 'There's no room for them to do that here, though,' she added, waving her hand around at all the junk. 'And we can't turn our cottage into a café because it isn't big enough.'

'But my shop *is* big enough!' said Cousin Ezra. ' I'm giving it to your mum. I don't want it now I'm moving to the city. I'll take all my junk with me, every single bit of it. You'll soon see how enormous the place is when I've taken all my junk away.'

Molly was excited and dismayed at the same time. Excited because they'd be able to stay here after all, dismayed in case . . .

'Not your top hat, Cousin Ezra!' said Molly, picking it up and peering down at Nipper who'd made himself quite at home inside it. 'You don't want to take the top hat, do you?' she asked anxiously.

'Perhaps I should,' said Cousin Ezra. 'It has turned out to be rather special.'

Nipper fluttered and flapped inside the hat and Molly peered down at him again. *'My wish is your command,'* Nipper said in a desperate-sounding voice.

'You . . . are you trying to tell me you're a . . . a . . . *genie?'* whispered Molly. 'If you are, why didn't you tell me before now?'

'My magic was fading. Most of my special magic got left behind in Miracle's top hat. I've put it in this top hat now, but I can't move it again! Sometimes my special magic makes me do things, sometimes it lets me tell things. Like

telling you, you have to make a wish before I can grant it,' Nipper replied.

'What? Oh, I get it!' Suddenly Molly remembered the first time Nipper had spoken was after she'd wished that he'd do something really magic – and she'd made that wish *after* Nipper had flown into Miracle's top hat.

Molly closed her eyes tight and wished: 'I wish Cousin Ezra would say we can have his grandfather's top hat!'

'On second thoughts,' Cousin Ezra said suddenly, 'Grandfather's top hat really belongs here at Pebbledown Bay. But just you make sure that you look after it,' he added,

waving a knobbly finger under Molly's
nose.

'All this nonsense about that old top hat!'
said Mum, shaking her head at Molly.
'Don't you realise we've got work to do?
We're going to turn this shop into a café
and make lots of money. We'll call the café
. . . Hinglepots' Comet . . .'

'Oh, I can't wait to tell Jack and Dad and
Gran and Pedro and the donkeys and
Miracle,' laughed Molly. 'I wish they were
all here.'

Suddenly the ground beneath their feet
started to shake and there was a loud sort
of explosive noise . . .

Seven

Jack and Dad and Gran, and Pedro and the donkeys, and Miracle burst through the door of the Junk Shop.

'*Slonkingpod*! I must be drowned,' said Dad Hinglepot who'd said if he ever set foot in the Junk Shop it would be over his drowned body.

'Three rows, Harold!' Gran's scarf had come with her and she thrust the end that was still being knitted into his hands.

'Olé! Olé!' shrieked Pedro. It was the only Spanish he knew – he told everyone he was Spanish but, really, he came from Liverpool.

'Eee-ore! Eee-ore!' brayed Bray and
Blare, talking back to Pedro.

'What am I doing here?' boomed Miracle
the Miraculous Magician. 'One minute I
was in New Pebbledown at the end of
the pier performing my miraculous
magic, next minute I'm here. I'll never dare
show my face there again, magician's
aren't supposed to make *themselves*
disappear!'

'Don't worry, Miracle,' said Mum

Hinglepot. 'As long as you help to get things ready, you can come and work in Hinglepots' Comet.'

'Oh, miracle,' boomed Miracle, 'I've always wanted to settle down, to stay in the same place all the time. I'll go and fetch all my worldly and unworldly goods!'

As Miracle miraculously disappeared, Mum said, 'That man will really help bring crowds to Hinglepots' Comet.'

'Emma, love,' said Dad sounding worried, 'I think some of that painted sand must have got into your brain. Even if you *have* discovered a new comet,' he added kindly, 'you won't be able to go there, you know!'

'I said she'd end up as crazy as Ezra spending so much time with him,' gloated Gran.

Mum laughed. '*This* is Hinglepots' Comet!' she said.

'B-b-b-but . . .' Dad Hinglepot gazed worriedly at his wife. 'I think we'd better send for a doctor,' he said, wiping his brow with a bit of the knitted scarf.

Mum ignored him and continued, 'At least, it will be. We've got lots of work to do first. And we've got to do it quickly so we can make lots of money before winter comes. I want Hinglepots' Comet open by this time next week! I'll phone the local newspaper and put a 'Grand Opening' announcement in.'

'B-b-but, Emma – '

'Harold!' said Mum. 'Please stop butting like a goat and listen to me . . .'

Jack was the only one who hadn't spoken. He wasn't listening to Mum, either. He was standing alone, all hunched and miserable. Molly went over to him.

'It's OK, Jack,' she told him. 'We can stay at Pebbledown Bay for ever and ever!

Listen to what Mum's saying. It's all true. I was here when Cousin Ezra said Mum could have the shop. We're going to turn it into a café. We'll have loads of holiday-making customers because of Mum's special recipes and because Miracle will be performing his miraculous magic here. Dad can take photographs to sell to the holiday-makers and we'll earn enough money to live on *and* to fix the roof.'

Jack started listening. 'Oh, wow!' he said. 'Oh, wow, Molly!'

Molly beamed and nodded. *And it's all thanks to Nipper*, she said silently. She'd decided to wait a while before telling Jack that Nipper was a genie. She wanted to be extra sure it wasn't a flash in a top hat, first!

Eight

The days passed quickly. Cousin Ezra had gone – taking all his junk with him and Hinglepots' Comet was taking shape. At least, it had been taking shape until Monday morning – the day before the 'Grand Opening' which had been advertised in the local newspaper.

On Monday morning, Bray and Blare decided to go looking for their best friends. Unfortunately, when the donkeys opened the café door and went inside, Miracle and all the Hinglepots were busy painting stars out the back while the *Red Giant Pies* were cooking in the oven.

And, upon not finding their best friends, Bray and Blare decided to sample the sea lavender which Molly and Jack had collected from Pebbledown Island for Mum's *Star-gazey Puddings*, the paper serviettes that Mum had spent hours folding into crescent moon shapes, and the menu cards as well!

It was Nipper who led to the discovery of the donkeys before they could open the oven and eat the *Red Giant Pies*. He picked up some painted stars in his claws and beak and flew inside with them. Molly ran after Nipper and her cries of dismay made everyone else run in after her.

Dad, earning a fine of ten rows of knitting for his *very* naughty words, chased Bray and Blare out. And Gran, chortling gleefully, went to find Pedro.

'We'll never be ready in time now!' said Mum in despair. And even if we could, I

can't make *Star-gazey Puddings* without sea
lavender.'

'And we can't go and fetch any more
because it's high tide,' said Jack.

'Dear lady,' Miracle boomed, doffing his
top hat. 'Shredded serviettes and mangled
menu cards are a magician's delight!'

Molly noticed Nipper beadily eyeing the
mangled menu cards, then shaking
his head.

Miracle murmured a few words and the pieces of shredded serviettes and mangled card floated round their heads before landing back on the tables as crescent moon-shaped serviettes and menu cards.

'But how startling!' murmured Mum, looking at the menu cards. *Star-gazey Puddings* isn't written on the menu cards now! There are green stars there instead! And they look like the constellation known as the Dragon. I think someone . . .' she smiled up at Miracle, '. . . is telling me that

I should be making *Dragon Delight Desserts* for our Grand Opening. If all of you will fill the salt and pepper pots and polish the cutlery and finish off painting the stars to decorate the tables, I'll go and make them now!'

Miracle looked puzzled as everyone got to work. Molly guessed he was wondering how the green stars had got onto the menu cards. But she knew and so did Nipper!

By the time Mum had made the desserts, Hinglepots Comet was almost ready for the next day.

'I just hope people will come!' Mum said nervously.

'There's no need to worry about that!' said Miracle, tapping the peculiar-looking bag he was holding.

The Hinglepots watched as Miracle pulled out a miraculously magical-looking name sign that got bigger and bigger

before their eyes, and had the words
Hinglepots' Comet flashing all over it in
millions of sizes and colours.

'This sign will flash and grow and dazzle
even more when we hang it over the door,'
Miracle boomed. 'Tourists in New
Pebbledown will see it and be drawn to it
like magic.'

'*Cronky-clarty*, can't you see it's too big to
get out through the door?' said Dad
Hinglepot. He was the tiniest bit jealous of
Miracle's miraculous magic! He '*cronky-*

clarted' again as Miracle waved his hands over the sign and shrunk it! Gran was so excited, she didn't say anything about a fine for using naughty words.

They all ran outside and Miracle hung the sign over the door. As soon as he'd put it up, it increased in size.

'It does look truly miraculous!' said Mum, smiling at Miracle.

'But what if it magically draws tourists here *now*?' said Dad, feeling jealous again.

'It will magically draw them here tomorrow!' said Miracle. 'So we'd better go back inside and put the finishing touches to everything.'

When they went back inside, Miracle muttered strange words over the menu cards. 'Just to help me help the customers get much more than they thought they'd ordered,' he boomed, winking at Jack and Molly.

Nine

Hinglepots' Comet was full to bursting for the 'Grand Opening'. And there were so many tourists outside – who'd been magically drawn by the sign from New Pebbledown – that the queue stretched right across Bray and Blare's field where Pedro was shrieking delightedly: 'Olé! Olé! Two donkey rides for the price of four!'

Dad buzzed round taking photographs of holiday-making tourists who'd managed to get inside, and all the newspaper reporters – who Mum had invited as her special guests – buzzed round taking photographs of Dad taking photographs.

As Molly, Jack and Gran served *Red Giant Pies*, *Dragon Delight Desserts* and *Milky Way Shakes*, Mum explained that Red Giant was the name given to any star when it got old. 'An old star swells up into a giant star, the surface cools off and makes the star looks red,' she said.

Then she smiled and added, 'And now,

here's another star. *Miracle the Miraculous Magician.'*

Miracle flourished his top hat and bowed deeply. 'I'm now going to perform miraculous magic on your *Red Giant Pies* and your *Dragon Delight Desserts*!' he said.

Molly heard Nipper *kyowing* excitedly from inside his top hat and she suddenly remembered something. Although she was extra sure Nipper was magic, she wasn't extra sure that he was a genie.

'I wish you'd do some starry magic, too!' she said.

Then, to his own surprise, when Miracle waved his magic wand, not only did *Red Giant Pies* grow bigger and redder and *Dragon Delight Desserts* roar loudly but . . . The *Milky Way Milk Shakes* fizzed with millions of stars.

'It was Nipper who did that,' Molly

whispered to Jack as everyone held up their star-fizzing drinks to congratulate the Hinglepots on the success of Hinglepots' Comet.

'You see,' Molly continued, 'Nipper isn't *just* magic, he's a genie too!'

'Huh! I wish I could believe that,' murmured Jack.

Nipper appeared on the brim of his top hat.

Jack gazed at the seagull.

Nipper gazed beadily back.

Then he said: '*Your wish is my command. But not yet . . . not quite yet . . .*'